TUFF FLUFF

The Case of Duckie's Missing Brain

SCOTT NASH

WALKER BOOKS
AND SUBSIDIARIES
LONDON · BOSTON · SYDNEY · AUCKLAND

3.29 a.m.

LOS ATTIC
A CITY THAT ALWAYS SLEEPS

My name is Flopsy Flips Rabbit™. But nobody with any sense calls me that. To them I'm Tuff Fluff, Private Investigator.

It all started when I was sitting in my office in the Ace Moving Box, workin' at *The Times* crossword puzzle. The watch on the wall said 3.29 a.m. It always said 3.29. I was looking for an eight-letter word for *fake medicine* that begins with a "Q" when I heard a soft thumping at my door.

"It's open!" I called.

I looked up and found myself staring at the business end of a fuzzy muzzle.

"Excuse me, Mr Fluff?" said the muzzle in a voice as thick and smooth as ketchup.

"That's me!" said me. "What's your name, big stuff?"

"My name is Bluebell. I need your help! Something terrible has happened. Could we talk … outside?"

I stepped outside to find that the muzzle was attached to the tallest stuffed teddy I'd ever seen. She was as big and blue as a whale in a room full of oranges.

"OK, Big Stuff, what's the problem?" I asked.

She says, "My friend Duckie is not ducky."

Something moved in the bear's shadow. Then out into the light stepped a yellow terry cloth duck.

"QUACK!" said the duck.

"Hmmmm, he seems pretty ducky to me," I said.

"But listen to him! All he does is quack," said the bear.

"QUACK!"

"Come here, Big Stuff," I said. "I have a secret for you." She bent down close, and I whispered into her velveteen ear, "He's a duck, sweetheart. Ducks quack."

"QUACK!"

"I beg your pardon," the bear said politely, "but stuffed ducks don't quack. They talk, just like you and me. My friend Duckie used to talk all the time."

"QUAAALK!"

squawked the duck.

"All right, I've got it, but I'm a detective, not a doctor!" I protested.

"Mr Fluff, I beg you, please take a look at my friend."

"All right, all right, I'll take a look," I said, as I pulled out my magnifying glass and inspected the duck from toe to head. There at the top of the poor duck's head was a split in the stitching and a dark gaping hole.

"Someone's been playing with this fowl," I said. "His brain's been lifted."

"You mean **STOLEN?**" she asked.

"Bingo!" I said. "But who would do such a terrible thing – and why?" (I could tell she was about to pop a stitch.)

"Relax, Ursa Major. I'm a detective. Before we can figure out the who and why, we need to investigate the where and when."

I locked the door to the office. "We gotta visit the scene of the crime. Take me to Duckie's place."

3.29 a.m.
later...

TO DUCKIE'S PLACE

We walked past noisy clock-works, plastic action figures and construction sets to Duckie's box of flats. It was a nice place on a quiet dead-end street near Beantown. That's the posh area of Los Attic.

"I'm too big to go inside. I'll wait out here," said the bear.

"Good idea! You stand guard and watch the box."

The hallway to Duckie's building was clean and well lit. So were the stairs. I counted four names on the door buzzer, including one Justin Duckie.

"Which floor?" I asked, as we began climbing the stairs.

"Quird!" said the duck.

When we reached the second floor landing, there was a CLICK and the lights went out. I set my feet and my fists, ready to knock the stuffing out of anything that attacked. The landing shook as something came barrelling down from the third floor and streaked past us, screaming,

"YIKE! YIKE! YIKE!"

"QUOOOCK! QUOOOCK!! QUOOOK!!!"

the duck hollered.

I gave chase, but whoever it was had already slipped out of the door and disappeared down the street. Big Stuff seemed to have disappeared too, which was a good trick for a three-storey-tall bear.

Just then I noticed something on the ground. I picked up the evidence with a handkerchief. "A bean!" I murmured, and tucked it safely in my pocket. Then I ran back upstairs.

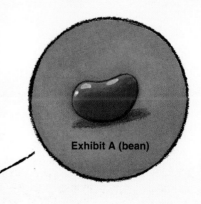

Exhibit A (bean)

Duckie's flat was a big place on the third floor with great views of the whole of Los Attic.

"Big Stuff!" I said with surprise and relief when I saw the bear's blue face through the window. "Where have you been?"

It turns out that the bear had been there the whole time with her face squished halfway in through a window at the side of the building, waiting for Duckie and me to enter his flat. So she'd missed all the excitement.

The flat was full of books. "For a fella with no brains, you're pretty bookie, Duckie!" I said.

That seemed to cause Duckie to snap altogether. He pulled a book off the table, threw it on the floor, and began quacking angrily at it. Poor guy.

I picked the book up. It was a swashbuckler called *The High-Seas Adventures of Blue Jay the Pirate.*

"We're not going to find the answer to this case in a book," I said, as I put it back on the table. "Let's find the beanbag that rolled past us and see if he spills."

And with that we ventured into the heart of Beantown.

3.29 a.m.

later still...

BEANTOWN

There was no love lost between beanbags and stuffs. To the beans, stuffs were riff-raff, the old toys. To us, beanbags were simply the newest batch of cast-offs. As we walked down the street we could feel the stares of itty-bitty beanie eyes watching us. Big Stuff cradled Duckie in her arms. The duck glared at something or someone ahead and growled.

"Try not to attract attention," I whispered. But it seemed Duckie had his own ideas about the situation. The words were hardly out of my mouth when the duck leapt from Big Stuff's arms and started madly chasing a caramel-coloured bulldog.

The dog barked a familiar

"YIKE! YIKE! YIKE!"

and slipped around the corner out of sight. Duckie followed in hot pursuit.

Soon the dog was back, this time with Duckie's bill clamped firmly to his beanie butt.

"QUERK! QUERK! QUERRRRRRRRK!"

growled the duck.

"Help! Get him off me!" cried the beanbag.

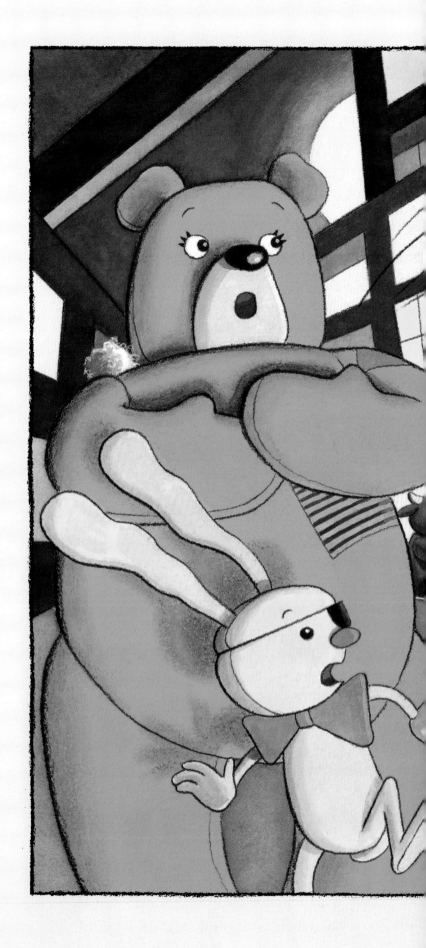

I prised Duckie off of the bulldog's tail, sat him up against a street lamp and looked him square in the eye. "Spill the beans, beanbag! Where's Duckie's brain!?"

"I don't know!" the beandog whimpered. "I don't even know what a duck brain looks like!"

I had no idea what a duck brain looked like either, but it wasn't a pretty thought so I changed the subject.

"All right then, why were you sneaking around Duckie's flat?"

"We were just lookin' for the stories!" he whined.

"We?" I looked up to find the whole street crawlin' with beanbags! They came in all styles and forms: polka-dotted giraffes, checked cats, paisley insects, chenille lizards. There was even a cute little flowered rabbit.

"Why don't you tell me your story?" I said to the beandog. "And start at the beginning."

The bulldog, known as Butter-bean, then told me how he and the rest of the beanbags used to listen in secret whenever Duckie was reading to Big Stuff:

"Every night the big bear here would show up at Duckie's place and stick her head in the top window. At first we were just curious about the bear, but then we heard the stories..."

"Mooving tales!" lowed a beancow.

"Such powerful oration!" an owl reminisced.

"So," I said, "you were all hiding out, listening to Duckie read. What next?"

"Well, that's about it. Then one night, we were listening in when all of a sudden Duckie just stopped readin' and started quackin'. When he wouldn't stop, the big blue bear started acting crazy.

We got scared, so we ran away."

"You're quite a story-teller yourself," I said to the dog as I helped him up. "You wouldn't happen to remember the title of the book Duckie was reading that night, would you?"

A kitten beanbag piped up and said, "It was about pirates!"

"TrrrrEASURE!" burped a frog.

"The high seas!" said a fish.

"Polly urgently needed a cracker," a parrot remembered.

"Hmmmm." I looked up at Big Stuff and winked. "I think we're close to solving this case," I said. "Let's go back to Duckie's place."

I turned to Butterbean. "You'd better come with us. Oh, and by the way, I believe this is yours," I said, and I handed him the bean from my pocket.

BACK TO DUCKIE'S

We made tracks back to Duckie's flat. There on the table, right where we had left it, was the book, *The High-Seas Adventures of Blue Jay the Pirate.*

I flipped through it until I came to the chapter with the title "In Which a Parrot Is Rescued from Certain Star-vation". There, between pages forty-four and forty-five, was a tuft of flattened fluff. "Behold!" I announced.

"Duckie's brain!"

Everyone rushed to see. "Stand back!" I hollered. But it was too late. The gust of air caused by the surge of onlookers made Duckie's fluffy brain shoot straight out of the book and into Big Stuff's gaping mouth! Big Stuff turned green and tried to cough it up. But soon we had to face facts: Duckie's brain was gone for good.

"QUAFFED!" squeaked Duckie weakly, and he crumpled to the floor.

"I feel queasy!" Big Stuff looked as if she was going to faint.

"It's OK, sweetheart. You'll be all right. Just have a seat and put your head down."

I have to admit, I was stumped. I didn't know what to do next. For a long minute I stood at the window and watched Big Stuff forlornly picking at the stuffing poking out of the holes in her threadbare fur.

"Stuffing! That's it!" I shouted. "Butterbean, stay here with Duckie. I'll be right back!"

Down on the street I said, "Big Stuff, I have a crazy idea that might save Duckie, but I need your help."

"Oh Tuff, I'd do anything for that little guy!" she cried.

"OK," I said, and took a deep breath. "Maybe all Duckie needs is some of your stuffing, if you can spare it."

Big Stuff smiled, stood up slowly and gently pulled tufts of stuffing from her body wherever she could find it until we had a big ball of fluff.

"Stand clear," I ordered, and I carried the precious stuff up the stairs to the flat, where Duckie was still out cold.

Butterbean and I attempted a rare and risky operation – a brain transplant in a stuffed duck.

"I need hot water, clean towels, a tray and a spoon!" Butterbean said to the beanbags assisting us.

I carefully set down the ball of fluff. Butterbean surprised me by placing his bean next to it.

"What's with this?" I says.

Butterbean solemnly explained, "Duckie is part beanbag to us. Our brains are beans. This might help."

So we filled Duckie's head with stuffing and a bean.

It wasn't pretty, but it worked like a charm. As soon as we were done, Duckie started talking nineteen to the dozen.

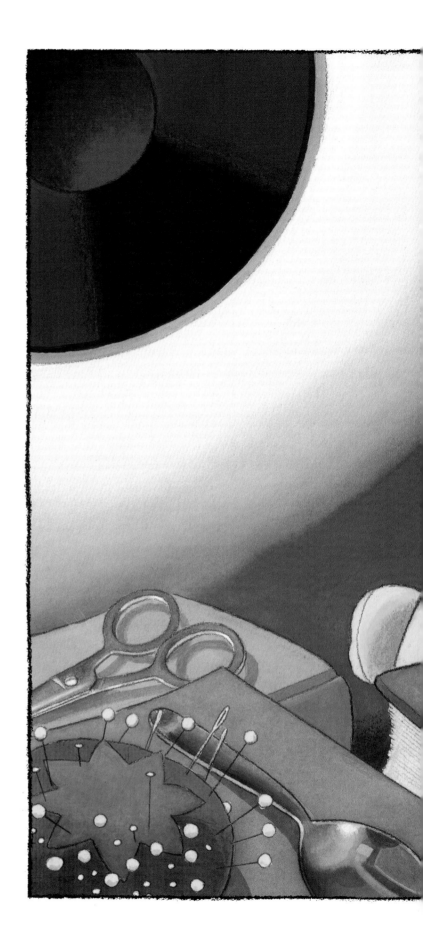

And so Duckie, smarter than ever, began to tell stories to an adoring audience of stuffs, beanbags and one very happy, slightly slimmer giant bear.

As for me, I only stayed for the beginning of the first chapter. Before I left, though, I got a hot tip for my crossword from that dexterous duck. "Duckie! What's an eight-letter word for *fake medicine*?"

Duckie lit up like a light bulb and said, "My dear Tuff, that would be *quackery*!"

3.29 a.m.
as usual

CASE CLOSED

I walked along the empty street back to my office, sat down at the desk and filled in the last word to complete the crossword puzzle.

I leant back in my chair and looked at the clock: 3.29, as usual. It was a quiet night in a city where beanbags and stuffs sat side by side, listening to stories.

Meanwhile, I'm in La-La Land dreaming up my own stories, starring Tuff Fluff, Rabbit Detective and his two partners, Duckie and Bluebell, alias Smart Fluff and Big Fluff.

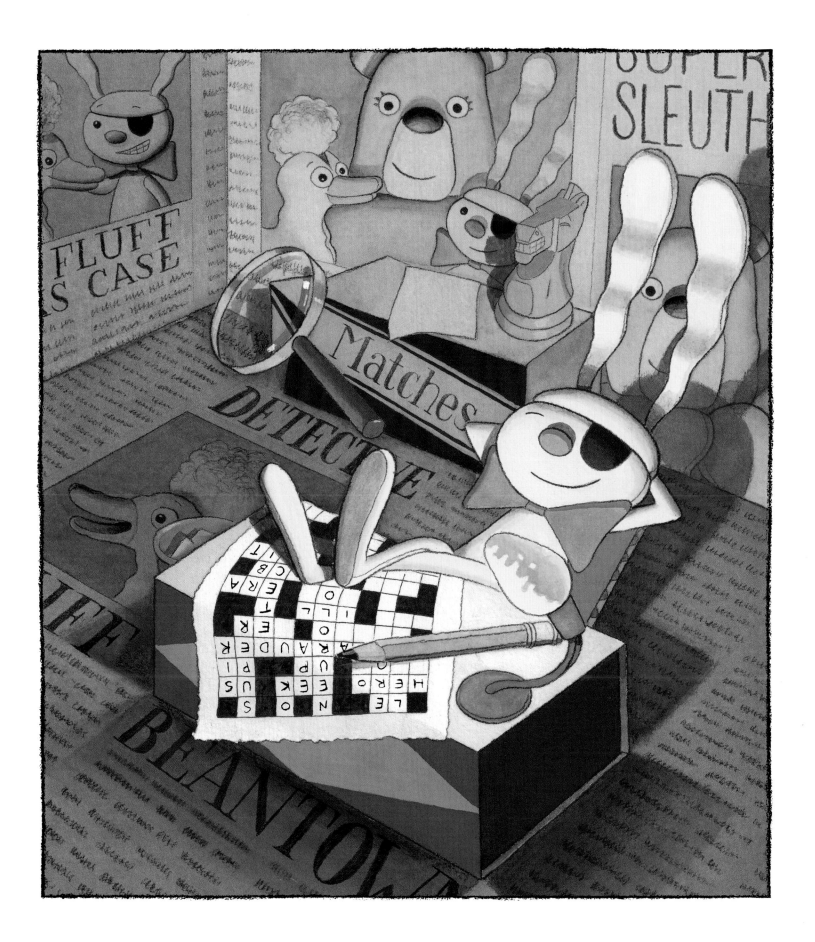